KU-303-361

There are lots of Early Reader
stories you might enjoy.

For a complete list, visit
www.hachettechildrens.co.uk

The Witch
of the Ditch

The Witch of the Ditch

Steven Butler

Illustrated by Nigel Baines

Orion
Children's Books

ORION CHILDREN'S BOOKS

First published in Great Britain in 2018
by Hodder and Stoughton

1 3 5 7 9 10 8 6 4 2

Text © Steven Butler 2018
Illustrations © Nigel Baines 2018

The moral rights of the author and illustrator have been asserted.

A CIP catalogue record for this book
is available from the British Library.

ISBN 978 1 5101 0193 7

Printed and bound in China

The paper and board used in this book are
made from wood from responsible sources.

MIX
Paper from
responsible sources
FSC® C104740
FSC
www.fsc.org

Orion Children's Books
An imprint of
Hachette Children's Group
Part of Hodder and Stoughton
Carmelite House
50 Victoria Embankment
London EC4Y 0DZ

www.hachette.co.uk
www.hachettechildrens.co.uk

For Francesca Simon
– S.B.

contents

chapter One

Every town in the world has one
witch. Exactly one! No more, no less.

There's no room for two witches in the same town. If two witches do live in the same town . . .

. . . their magic gets all muddled up,
they get jealous and competitive, and
it always ends in . . . well . . . you'll
see in a minute.

It was last Tuesday morning when Elsie (**The Witch of the Ditch**) opened the backdoor of her crooked cottage and stepped out into the sunshine.

She stood there, as short and round as a barrel in pyjamas, and smiled a wonky smile.

'Looks like the perfect day for casting spells,' she cackled to her pet dog, Bruce. 'I want to try turning cowpats into cake!'

Elsie stretched and yawned
and was about to start
looking for a nice, sturdy
cowpat, when she smelled a
strange whiff of something
on the wind.

It was a smell she knew
very well . . .

It was the smell of **MAGIC!**

Chapter Two

Elsie looked at Bruce.

The smell of magic was a very normal thing to be hanging around a witch's house, but Elsie hadn't used any magic yet that morning.

Something wasn't quite right. Elsie went inside to investigate.

'Have you been messing about near my potions again, Bruce?' she asked.

Bruce rolled onto his back and wagged his tail.

'Hmmm . . .'

If Bruce hadn't knocked over any potions, and Elsie hadn't started casting spells, that must mean . . .

SOMEONE ELSE WAS USING MAGIC!

With a flick of her wand, Elsie was dressed. She snatched her flying goggles from their peg by the kitchen door and grabbed her broom from the corner.

WHOOOOOSH! Elsie mounted her broomstick and rocketed out through the kitchen window.

Up, up, up Elsie flew, high into the air. She looked down at her cottage in the ditch, just outside a small town, on the side of a steep mountain.

Elsie shot higher and higher
until the rooftops were as small
as postage stamps beneath her.
That's when she saw it.

On the mountain peaks above the town, purple lightning was crackling and there were great puffs of smoke coming from a cottage.

'There never used to be a cottage here,' she gasped. **'FLY, broom, FLY!'**

With that, **The Witch of the Ditch** whizzed straight to the front door of the strange, new cottage and banged on it loudly.

chapter Three

'Who's disturbing **The Hag of the crag?**' came a voice from inside.

'**IT'S ME, THE WITCH OF THE DITCH!**' Elsie bellowed. '**OPEN UP!**'

The front door opened and a tall, thin witch with rainbow-coloured clothes and enormous glasses stepped outside.

They stared at each other for a moment.

'This is my town,' said Elsie. 'You can't live here.'

'Rubbish!' said **The Hag of the Crag**. 'This is my town. YOU can't live here.'

The Hag of the crag waved her wand and turned Elsie's pointed hat into frogspawn.

SPLAT! The frogspawn ran down Elsie's face and plopped all over her shoes.

'RUBBISH!' yelled Elsie. She flicked her wand and **The Hag of the Crag's** cardigan unravelled in a ball of wool. It bounced on the ground and rolled down the garden path.

'That's done it!' hissed **The Hag of the crag**. 'Witch fight!'

'What?' asked Elsie.

'A witch fight,' said **The Hag of the crag**.

'Using our best spells, whoever can make the other witch hopping mad by dinnertime, wins. The winner gets to stay. The loser has to pack up and move someplace else. DEAL?'

'Deal!' said Elsie. She had some fantastic spells up her sleeve. There was no way she could fail.

'Fine,' said **The Hag of the Crag**. She tapped her wand on the end of Elsie's stubby nose.

POP! There was a huge puff of smoke and Elsie found herself standing back in her kitchen in the ditch.

'Bruce!' Elsie yelled. 'Fetch the spell book. We've got work to do.'

chapter Four

By noon, Elsie had conjured up a huge, green cloud that floated above **The Hag of the Crag's** cottage and rained Brussels sprouts.

'Haha! That should do the trick!' she chuckled.

But at 1:00 p.m., Elsie's plates and cups and knives and forks all flew out of the kitchen cupboards and dipped themselves in the mud-bog outside the window.

Then they flew inside and stacked themselves back in the cupboard, covered in slime.

Elsie could hear **The Hag of the Crag** cackling from high up on the mountain.

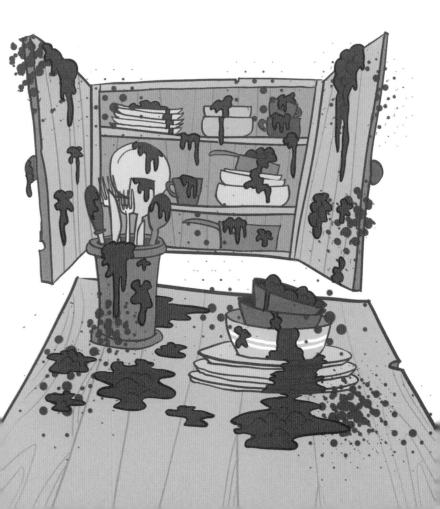

'She's not going to make me hopping mad that easily,' said Elsie. She ran outside, jabbed her wand in the direction of the craggy cottage, and turned all of The Hag's furniture into jelly.

'**BLUUUUHHH!**' came a screech
from the top of the mountain.

By 2:00 p.m., Elsie's hair had turned bright pink, and **The Hag of the Crag's** skin was covered in pimples.

By 3:00 p.m., the weeds in Elsie's ditch-garden had all turned into dragon flowers. They gnashed their teeth and shook their thorns, spitting fire every time Elsie opened the back door.

By 4:00 p.m., **The Hag of the Crag** had sprouted itchy fur and a long puffy tail. The Hag couldn't help but scratch and howl like a wild animal.

As the hours rolled on, things got worse. By 7:30 p.m., the people of the town had all run inside their houses to hide from the explosions of magic above them.

The two witches were facing each other on their broomsticks now, high up in the sky.

'Bog off!' yelled Elsie, as she turned **The Hag of the Crag's** nose into a cactus.

'No, you!' **The Hag of the Crag** yelled back, as she summoned up a flock of birds to poop on Elsie's jumper.

'That's it!' they both screamed. At exactly the same time, **The Witch of the Ditch** and **The Hag of the Crag** pointed their wands at each other and . . . **CRACKLE! FIZZ! BOOM!**

chapter Five

The magic spells crashed into each other. There was a brilliant flash of lightning and then both their broomsticks turned into spaghetti.

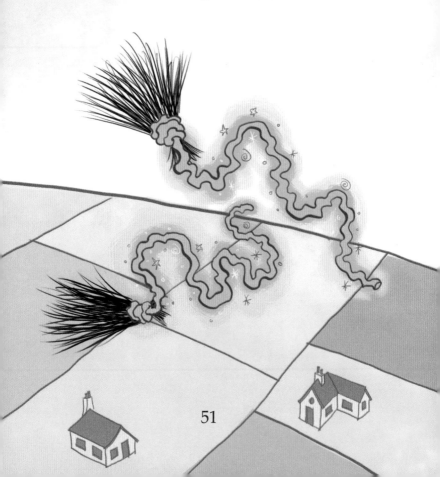

51

'AAAAAAAGGHH!'

Down, down, down the two
witches fell until . . .

'SPLOOOOSH!'

They both landed in the fountain at the edge of the town square.

'Ugh!' Elsie clambered to her feet.
She was dripping wet and her
hair was stuck all over her face.

The Hag of the Crag sat up in the water and looked at Elsie.

'So who won?' Elsie asked.

'I did!' said **The Hag of the crag.**

'No, I did!' said Elsie.

Just then the ground started to shake. A huge crack opened up in the middle of the town square.

'Stop casting spells!' snapped **The Hag of the crag.**

'It's not me,' said Elsie, holding up her broken wand.

A cottage rose up out of the great, big hole in the ground. For a moment there was silence, until the front door opened and a witch stepped out.

'Who are you?' asked Elsie,
clambering out of the fountain.

'I am **The Wench of the Trench**,' said the new witch. 'This is my town. You two can't live here.'

The **Witch of the Ditch** and **The Hag of the Crag** looked at each other.